Poppy's Big Push

Victorian stories linking with the History
National Curriculum.

First published in 1996 by Franklin Watts
96 Leonard Street, London EC2A 4RH

© Mary Hooper 1996

The right of Mary Hooper to be identified as
the Author of this Work has been asserted by
her in accordance with the Copyright, Designs
and Patents Act, 1988

Series editor: Paula Borton
Consultant: Joan Blyth
Designed by Kirstie Billingham

A CIP catalogue record for this book
is available from the British Library.

ISBN 0 7496 2361 6

Dewey Classification 941.081

Printed in Great Britain

Poppy's Big Push

by
Mary Hooper

Illustrations by Lesley Bisseker

W
FRANKLIN WATTS
LONDON · NEW YORK · SYDNEY

1

Nag! Nag! Nag!

"You country girls are green behind the ears!" the housekeeper said crossly, coming up behind Poppy and tugging one of her plaits quite hard. "I don't know what the mistress is thinking of, taking you on. Why, I don't suppose you've ever seen a kitchen range before, let alone cleaned one!"

Poppy was facing away from the housekeeper, bending over the huge black kitchen range and raking out the ashes. She pulled a face. No, she hadn't seen a kitchen range before - come to that, she hadn't seen a proper kitchen - but she wasn't going to let the housekeeper know

that. Being the youngest of fifteen staff working at Knightley House for Lord and Lady Throckmorten, Poppy got quite enough teasing as it was.

"I told you yesterday – the range must be cleaned, black-leaded and lit before six o'clock!" the housekeeper ranted. "If the fire isn't going by then, the water won't be hot enough for the family to have their washing water taken up at eight."

"Yes, Ma'am," Poppy said, her face going almost as red as her hair with the effort of not answering back.

"And once the water's boiled, Cook and I want our pot of tea brought up at seven on the dot!" the ranting continued. "Not five or six minutes past like it was today."

Poppy nodded.

"And if you should happen to see a member of the family while you're going about your duties you disappear, do you understand? Just disappear." She gave a shudder. "No one wants to see a scullery maid."

She gave Poppy's other plait a tug for good measure and strode away, the keys of the larders clanking. She was an ugly, bony woman, as tall and thin as Cook was short and fat. Neither of them spoke to Poppy except to shout at her - but then nor did the parlour maids, the ladies' maids, the housemaids or the menservants. If it wasn't for Hannah, the kitchen maid she shared a

room with, no one would speak to her at all. Poppy had discovered that she really missed her sisters - actually missed Lily and Rose and Marigold and little Daisy, even though all they'd done was squabble when she'd lived at home. Working in a big house in London wasn't as exciting as she'd imagined it would be. All you did was work and sleep – there was no time for anything else.

Poppy twisted the golden key on its string round her neck, thinking that there certainly hadn't been time to hunt for the treasure that the key was supposed to lead to...

"You, girl, clear these trays!" one of the housemaids called, coming down with two trays of breakfast dishes from upstairs. Poppy left the range and ran to take them from her.

"Miss Isabella threw a tantrum about the porridge," the housemaid reported with satisfaction to Cook. "Said it wasn't creamy enough."

Poppy's ears pricked up. She was the same age as the Honourable Isabella

Throckmorten, the daughter of the house, so she was always interested in hearing bits of gossip about her.

"I don't suppose that new governess will last two minutes," one of the parlour maids said. "She's much too meek. Miss Isabella will make mincemeat of her, just like she did the last one."

"Spoilt br—" the housemaid began, and then spotted Poppy listening and pursed her lips firmly together.

"Get on with those breakfast things, you!" Cook shouted, and Poppy scuttled away into the scullery

with its two big, deep sinks containing what seemed to be endless washing up.

She ran the tap, reached for the washing soda and marvelled for the umpteenth time at having water coming out of a tap, without having to go to the well for it. Mind you, she thought, if she had to walk to the well then at least she'd be getting out somewhere, instead of being stuck in the scullery all day.

2

A Morning Call

The rain beating on the windows woke Poppy early the next day and she stared around her. Although she'd been at the house some weeks now, she still hadn't got used to having so much space. At home she'd shared the bedroom and two small beds with five sisters and brothers - and behind the curtain there had been Ma and Dad and the baby as well - but here she and Hannah had a whole big room just to themselves.

She looked at the furniture proudly – she had a table and chest of drawers and wardrobe of her own, and it hardly mattered that they didn't have much in them.

There was a carpet of sorts, too (Poppy had never seen one before) and wall hangings with words from the Bible and pictures of lambs skipping, a garden of flowers and fat cherubs looking out of a cloud. Poppy liked this one best – the cherubs reminded her of Daisy.

She raised herself on one elbow and looked out of the window. London was out there – rows and rows of houses and masses of people and shops and theatres and restaurants. She'd also heard there were pleasure parks with music and dancing, but she had no hope of ever getting to them.

There was a groan and a sigh from Hannah in the other bed and Poppy realised it was time to get up. She sleepily made her way to the washstand, splashed her face in the cold water she'd brought up the night before and put on her uniform – a long, blue-checked dress with a white collar and white apron. She'd been given three sets of these by the housekeeper. They were all too big for her, but Poppy was used to clothes being big enough for her to grow into, so didn't really mind.

She walked down the back stairs to the basement, lifting her dress delicately by two points, as she'd seen the Honourable Isabella doing. In the kitchen, all was dark and quiet. She'd found it creepy at first, so silent and shadowy, but there were so many things to do, and to be done so quickly, that she just had to get on and do them and try not to think about the creepiness.

It was at this time of day that she missed Ma and the family the most. At home in the cottage there would be noise and bustle, with Daisy crying to be fed, Dad and the boys wanting their hunks of bread and ale before they set out for work, the twins squabbling and everyone stumbling around bumping into each other. Here it was just shadows and stillness.

As Poppy was bending over the range clearing out the ashes, the sudden clanging of a bell made her jump and she ran over to see who was calling down for a maid.

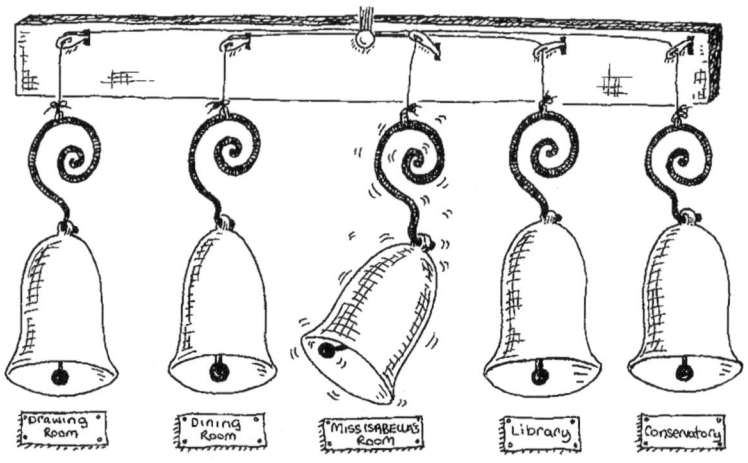

Miss Isabella's room! Poppy pulled a face, she'd just have to wait until one of the housemaids came down.

The bell continued to clang, demanding attention, and Poppy sighed and wiped her sooty hands on her apron.

Knowing Miss Isabella's reputation she'd wake the whole household if someone didn't go and see what she wanted. But where, exactly, was her room?

It took a good five minutes for Poppy to find Miss Isabella's second-floor bedroom – and she only found it then because the Honourable Miss was standing at her bedroom door stamping her foot.

"I've been ringing down for half an hour!" she stormed. "My window's been rattling all night and I haven't had a wink of sleep. I want someone to—"

She stopped and frowned at Poppy. "Who are you?"

Poppy bobbed a curtsy. "The new scullery maid, Miss."

"The scullery maid!" Isabella said with horror. "How dare someone dirty like you come upstairs! Didn't anyone tell you that kitchen staff aren't allowed on this floor? Get back there immediately and—"

But Poppy was already going crossly towards the back stairs. If that's what you got for trying to help, she thought, then she jolly well wouldn't bother again.

3

A Grand Banquet

"Madam is interviewing for a governess for Miss Isabella this afternoon," Hannah confided to Poppy as they chopped vegetables in the scullery ready for the staff lunch. "Apparently the new one's leaving."

"Already?" Poppy said.

"She stayed two months," Hannah said. "That's longer than some."

"I thought she was nice," Poppy said, for although the governess had, of course, taken her meals in the housekeeper's dining room with the senior staff, she had made a point of talking to Poppy. She'd given her some books and encouraged her with her reading, which had got much better. She was so good, in fact, that she was reading one of Mr Dickens' serials, *David Copperfield*, to the lower staff on a Sunday evening after Church.

"You're right, she was nice," Hannah said tartly, "too nice. That's why she was no good at dealing with the little minx upstairs."

"You two in there – stop the chattering. Are those vegetables done?" Cook roared from the kitchen. "We want to eat at midday sharp. There'll be no time to spare this afternoon."

Poppy and Hannah rolled their eyes at each other. The Throckmorten family were throwing a special dinner that evening in honour, the staff had been told, of the opening of the Great Exhibition. Poppy didn't know what this was, all she knew was that forty people were sitting down for a meal and most were staying the night, and everything was panic and pandemonium.

By nine o'clock that evening Poppy, who'd been on the go for over fifteen hours, was exhausted. It wouldn't have been so bad if they got any thanks, Poppy thought, but Cook was in a foul mood and not the least bit grateful. Why, she and Hannah only had to put their heads out of the scullery to be yelled back into it.

Some of the other maids were exhausted, too – but not due to plain tiredness. That evening, to Cook's horror, one after the other they went down with headaches and tummy aches and were sent to their beds. By the time the dinner party was in full swing, the house was down to only six waiting staff.

Cook and the housekeeper didn't know what to do, but in the end the butler said there was nothing else for it, Poppy would have to help by carrying the desserts upstairs.

A long black dress and white lace apron were quickly found. Poppy's face and hands were scrubbed, her plaits coiled up under a lace cap. The remaining staff who had a moment to spare looked Poppy up and down.

"She cleans up all right," Jack, one of the young footmen, said.

"You'd never know she was a scullery maid," said someone else with approval.

"Miss Isabella has her hair up for the first time tonight, too," said the butler.

Poppy wished she had a moment to see herself in a mirror, but there was no time to spare. She was given a tray of cream custards and told to step inside the door of the dining hall, place the tray on the side table and leave immediately.
On no account was she to linger, or even look at the guests.

Wildly excited, eyes lowered, Poppy entered the great dining hall of Knightley House. She placed the tray safely down on the polished sideboard and, heaving an inward sigh of relief, took a quick, forbidden look about the room as she made her way out.

The sight before her made her gasp. The long table was laid with silver and gold dishes, sparkling glass, pyramids of fruit and tumbling masses of flowers. And the food! Poppy had never seen so much. There were jellies, creams and blancmanges, and candied fruits shimmered in the glow from the gas lights and candles.

The guests sparkled and shimmered too. The ladies wore fancy crinoline dresses with tucks and bows and the men wore silk or satin suits in rich colours.

But Poppy's eye was caught by one man in particular. His suit was deep, midnight blue and he had a heavy gold watch chain dangling from his embroidered waistcoat.

When she saw the watch, Poppy stopped dead in her tracks, for on it was the four-leaved clover that had been on the gold locket Ma had owned. Inside that watch, Poppy knew, would be another clue to finding the treasure.

4

Another Clue

"Great-Grandma was very rich, you see," Poppy said to Hannah as they waited to take up another tray of desserts.

"It all sounds like a bit of a fairy story to me," Hannah said with a yawn.

"It's not!" Poppy said. "Ma told me

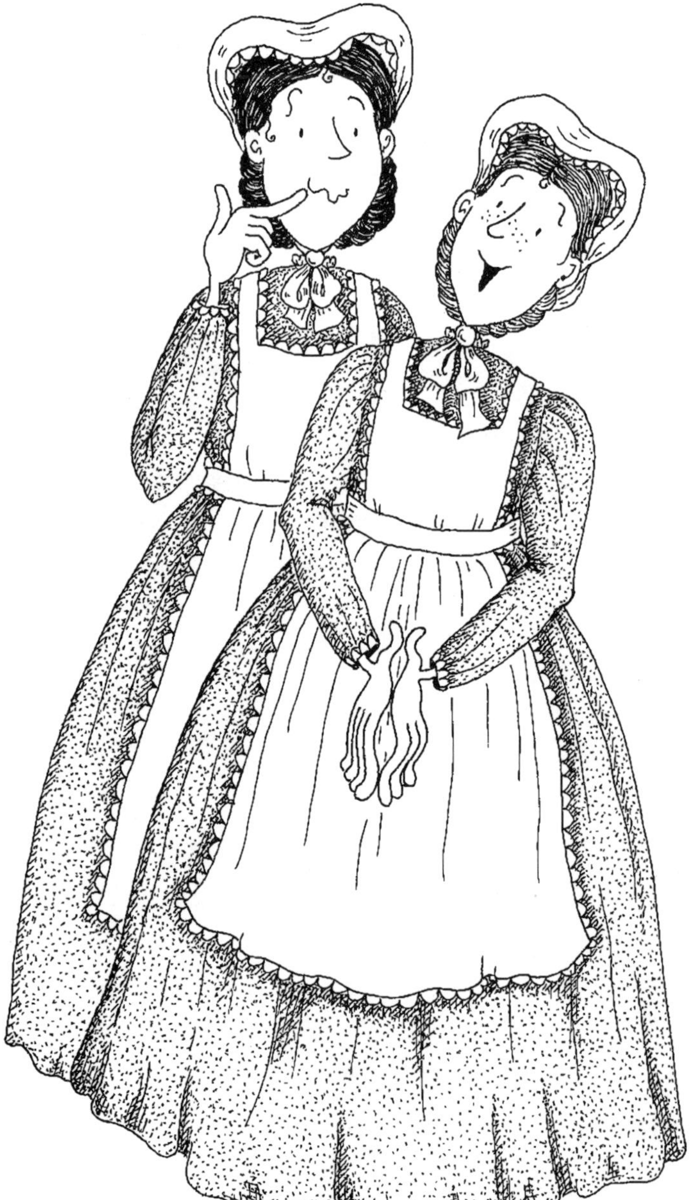

about it when I was little. Great-Grandma had four children, there was a big row and they all fell out, so she hid her money away so they wouldn't get it unless they made friends."

"How did she do that?"

"Well," Poppy said, "she gave each of them either a locket or a pocket watch with one line of a riddle engraved inside."

"And you know your line?"

Poppy nodded. "And if I find the other three it will lead to the treasure and then I can buy Ma and Dad a big house and we'll never be poor again!"

Hannah snorted.

Poppy's eyes glinted. "So I've just got to look inside that watch upstairs."

❖

On Poppy's third visit to the dining room - to take in dishes of tiny chocolates decorated with marzipan - she was lucky. It was getting late and the ladies were preparing to leave the room so that the gentlemen could smoke. When Lady Throckmorten asked what the hour was, three men got out their pocket watches and clicked them open. In a second, Poppy was by the side of the gentleman in blue, offering him a plate of chocolates.

This was strictly against orders, but she felt reckless enough not to care.

The line of the riddle was engraved there. She could see it! She bent eagerly over his shoulder to read it – and then heard a shriek of anger from the Honourable Isabella.

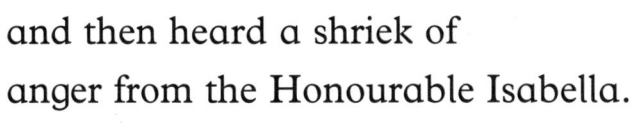

"It's that scullery maid again! How dare you stand and gawp at our guests. Mama!"

On the first word Poppy was making for the door, and by the last she was halfway down the hall, repeating what she'd read to herself and trying to make sense of it.

"Did you get what you wanted?" Hannah asked when she reached the kitchen.

Poppy nodded breathlessly. Together, this is what the first two lines of the riddle say:

Where life's torch flames burn no more
And the urn is covered o'er.

Hannah looked at her blankly. "What does that mean?"

Poppy shrugged. "I don't know. I've got to find the other two lines of the riddle for it all to make sense. And I will, someday…"

5

Sunday Best

"Master is exhibiting at the Great Exhibition, of course," Jack said at breakfast the following Sunday morning.

"What is the Great Exhibition?" Poppy asked.

"Don't you know?" Jack said scornfully.

"Why, the whole of London's talking about it."

Hannah sniffed. "Well, we don't hear much London gossip down here," she said, "so you'd better tell us."

"It's to show off England's cleverness," Jack said, glad of the opportunity to show off his own. "It's furniture and machines and discoveries and new gadgets and the like all under one roof. They've put 'em in a great big glass house they call the Crystal Palace."

"The Crystal Palace..." Poppy said wonderingly. "I'd like to see that."

"So what's the master got there?" Hannah asked.

"Oh, some new invention from his mill," said Jack. "Something or other which makes the looms go faster."

"I didn't know he had a mill," said Poppy.

"Oh, he's got a mill all right," said a parlour maid. "He's very rich, is Master. He's got a farm, four houses and a big mill near Morchester."

"Morchester!" Poppy said, "that's where my family live." She felt a great pang of homesickness and went very quiet.

As it was Sunday, all staff were expected to attend Church morning and afternoon. The Throckmortens went too – but they were in the downstairs pews at the front, of course, while Poppy and the servants were in the upstairs balcony.

After she'd cleared away the staff breakfast things and washed up, Poppy went to get changed for Church into the one frock she had with her – a washed-out navy blue cotton dress she'd arrived in from home. When she went downstairs again, the senior parlour maid looked at her and frowned.

"Haven't you anything better?" she asked. "In London, we wear our Sunday best to Church, you know."

Poppy shook her head. "This is what I came in," she said. She swung her bonnet by a frayed ribbon. "This and my bonnet."

"Can't we find her some cast-offs of Miss Isabella's?" the head parlour maid asked the housekeeper. "It's really too much to expect senior staff to walk along with someone so..." she looked delicately down her nose, "so ill-dressed."

"Miss Isabella did throw out her white cotton frock," the housekeeper said. "Now that she's got her hair up she says she's too grown up for white cotton. Besides, fashionable ladies are wearing crinolines." The white dress (which Cook had been hoping to take for her niece) was fetched from the rag bag and quickly examined. It was much too wide for Poppy, but when a sash borrowed from Hannah was tied tightly round the waist, it fitted her perfectly.

"And much better than that ragged thing," the head parlour maid said warmly.

New ribbons were tied onto Poppy's bonnet to match the sash, and when the staff set off, two-by-two, to walk to Church, it was a very fine-looking Poppy who brought up the rear. Jack the footman whistled in a vulgar way when he saw her and had to be cuffed by the butler. Poppy herself thought it was the most beautiful frock in the world, and far and away the nicest thing she'd ever owned. If Lily and Rose could only see her now!

But her glory didn't last long. The service was over and soon everyone was home and back in uniform. As they were preparing lunch for the family, a message came down that the housekeeper was wanted upstairs.

She came back five minutes later with her mouth set in a tight line.

"Miss Isabella," she announced, "doesn't want her clothes to be worn by a scullery maid. She has decided she wants the frock back."

Poppy gave a little squeal of dismay.

"Well, how mean!" Hannah exclaimed. "It's because Poppy looked so pretty in it."

"That's quite enough," the housekeeper said. "You, Miss, don't question your betters."

"It must be returned now," she added and Poppy, sighing, went upstairs to get the white frock. Miss Isabella might be her better, she thought, but she was perfectly hateful.

Ma and Pa Harding,
5 Railway Cottages,
Morchester.

6

Poppy's Big Push

Dearest Ma,

I was happy to hear I have a new brother and that he has red hair like me. I think Albert is a very good name.

I got a tip from a tradesman and I am using it to buy a stamp to send this to you.

Jack the footman said he would take it to the post office for me and use the Penny Post.

Everything is very grand here. In the kitchen there is water out of a tap, and upstairs there is a privy with a chain that you pull so that water comes down like a waterfall, making a great noise.

I am getting on all right but I miss everyone badly.

I wish I could see your new cottage and would love to see Baby Albert. Please give my love to Lily, Rose, Marigold, Alfred, George and especially Daisy.

I have another line to the riddle! A very grand gentleman here was wearing the watch and I looked inside it.

From your loving Poppy.
P.S. There is something called the Great Exhibition here which sounds very exciting but is not for the like of servants and I doubt whether I shall see it.

But that was where Poppy was wrong.

That day, the Throckmorten family were lunching with friends before going on to the Great Exhibition. During the day a wind blew up, making the Honourable Isabella feel slightly chilly. She asked that her warm cloak be collected from the house.

As luck would have it, the servants who'd recovered from their recent sickness were busy and it was up to Poppy to take the cloak to Hyde Park. She was given directions to where Miss Isabella and her Mama would be waiting, and told to wear Hannah's best blue serge coat to make sure she looked decent.

It was with great excitement that
Poppy, wearing the over-large coat, set off
with the cloak wrapped in tissue paper.
Catching the horse-drawn omnibus was
adventure enough, but when Poppy drew
near to the Great Exhibition
she found she could
barely breathe.
She was so
thrilled at
the sight of
thousands
of people

flocking through Hyde Park towards the enormous fairy castle glittering before them. Poppy was so amazed and dazzled that she allowed herself to be swept along with the crowd right up to the great doors. Then she had to fight her way back to reach the statue where she was supposed to meet Miss Isabella.

But the Honourable Miss Isabella had been parted from her adoring Mama and, because she'd had to wait, was rather cross.

She was so cross, in fact, that she was stamping around muttering about servants *always* being late and didn't notice that a horse, frightened by the crowd, had bolted and was dragging its carriage towards her at a frightening speed.

Poppy
peered
around
the statue
and saw the horse
before Miss Isabella did. As the driver
screamed a warning, Poppy dropped the
cloak and jumped at Miss Isabella,
knocking her to the ground but also
knocking her out of the way of the horse.

For a moment both were flat on the
ground, breathless.

"How...dare..."
Miss Isabella began, gathering breath to scream, but from all around people came running, saying what a lucky escape she'd had and how her life had been saved.

Miss Isabella fell completely silent for a moment, then stared at Poppy with wide eyes, burst into tears and called for her Mama.

❖

The whole event was hushed up, on account of it not being thought right to be knocked to the ground by your scullery maid, but Poppy greatly enjoyed telling the other servants the tale. Later that evening, she was called to Miss Isabella's room and presented with a parcel containing three dresses, a wool cloak and a pink taffeta bonnet with matching gloves.

The talk she had with Miss Isabella pleased Poppy even more than the new clothes.

For she learnt that, the season in London was almost over and the whole household would shortly be moving to the house near to Lord Throckmorten's mill in Morchester.

The awkward conversation finished (Miss Isabella had never had to talk to a scullery maid before) and Poppy carefully carried the new clothes upstairs to her wardrobe. Then she counted the number of dresses she had.

After that she got out the letter to Ma and added another P.S.

Ma, I went to the Great Exhibition today and saved Miss Isabella's life. I will be able to tell you about it shortly, for I have just learned that we will soon be going to Morchester. I shall be living near you and Miss Isabella says I may visit once a month. Much love from your very happy daughter, Poppy.

Victorian Life

Domestic servants

Working as a servant in a big house was just about the only job available for a girl like Poppy who was poor and had not had much education. A servant would work for up to 16 hours a day, be paid very little and would be nagged by just about everyone! They would get time off on Sundays to go to Church but would usually only be allowed to go home to see their families just one day a year - on Mothering Sunday.

Charles Dickens

Charles Dickens was a great author of the Victorian Age who wrote books which were not only exciting stories but also talked about how poor and unhappy many people were at the time. They were usually published one chapter at a time and were eagerly read by his fans. The stories were followed in the same way that people follow, say, *Coronation Street* or *EastEnders* today.

The Great Exhibition

Queen Victoria's husband, Prince Albert, was the brains behind the Great Exhibition in 1851. It was held in a huge, wonderful, glass and iron building nicknamed the "Crystal Palace". It contained 16 kilometres of exhibits and was set up to show that Britain was the best in the world at designing and making things. Over six million people came to the Great Exhibition, many visiting London for the first and only time in their lives.

Penny Post

From 1840 onwards, you could buy a one penny stamp, and this would take a letter anywhere in Britain. Before this, the person you wrote to had to pay for the letter when they got it. If they couldn't afford to pay then the letter would be sent back to you!

The lavatories of London

During Victoria's reign, people began to realise that dirty water spread disease, so they began to build sewers and some of the richer people had running water systems. The Throckmorten's house actually had a flush lavatory, but only the family were allowed to use it. The staff had to use the tin shed outside in the yard.